Panda Bear Cub

by Jacqueline Moody-Luther

Illustrated by Will Nelson

Little®
Soundprints

To Jackson Race, my curly-headed cub. I live for your bear hugs. — J.L.

For my three girls, Kris, Cori, and Holly — W.N.

Book design: Marcin Pilchowski
Editor: Ben Nussbaum
Production Editor: Brian E. Giblin

First Edition 2006
10 9 8 7 6 5 4 3 2 1
Printed in China

Acknowledgments:
Our very special thanks to Dr. Don E. Wilson of the Department of Systematic Biology at the Smithsonian Institution's National Museum of Natural History for his curatorial review.
Soundprints would also like to thank Ellen Nanney and Katie Mann at the Smithsonian Institution's Office of Product Development and Licensing for their help in the creation of this book.

Library of Congress Cataloging-in-Publication Data is on file with the publisher and the Library of Congress.

Panda Bear Cub

by Jacqueline Moody-Luther

Illustrated by Will Nelson

A note to the reader:
Throughout this story you will see words in **bold letters**. There is more information about these words in the glossary. The glossary is in the back of the book.

On a warm summer day in a **bamboo** forest, Panda Bear Cub is born. She is very tiny and pink.

Cub grows so fast.
Soon she is black
and white. She is
still not able to see.

Mother and Cub
live in a **den** in a
hollow tree trunk.
Bamboo is all
around the tree.

When she is six
weeks old, Cub
finally opens her
eyes. The first
thing she sees
is Mother!

It is cold and
damp. But today
is a special day
for Cub. She walks
for the first time!

Soon, Cub can go with Mother when she collects bamboo to eat. Cub wants to **explore** her world.

One day, Cub

sees some birds.

She walks toward

the chirping noises.

The birds fly away.

Where is Mother?

Cub is lost!

Cub hears a **crackling** in the bamboo. It is Mother! Cub covers her eyes with her front paws. Cub is sorry she wandered off.

Cub is glad to be near her mother. They walk through the snow, finding bamboo to eat.

Someday, Cub will make a home of her own. But for now, she is happy to stay with her mother in the bamboo forest that is their home.

Glossary

Bamboo: A type of thick grass that panda bears like to eat.

Crackling: A snapping, breaking noise.

Den: A small, comfortable area where animals live.

Explore: To travel and search in new areas.

About Panda Bears

Panda bears live in western China. Bamboo is their main source of food and they live in forests where it grows. Panda bears spend 12 to 16 hours a day eating!

Pandas are about the same size as black bears and live for about 25 years. They are white with black patches. Pandas are slow-moving bears and do not hibernate. They have giant claws, allowing them to climb trees to escape enemies or seek shelter.

The Chinese believed that pandas could ward off natural disasters and evil spirits through their magical powers. Chinese emperors even kept them as pets. The Chinese name for panda bears means giant cat bear. This might be because panda bears cannot walk on their hind legs and must use all four legs when they walk.

Other animals that live near panda bears:

Bamboo rats

Golden takins

Clouded leopards

Siberian rubythroats

Golden monkeys